★ *GREAT SPORTS TEAMS* ★

THE CLEVELAND

INDIANS

BASEBALL TEAM

David Pietrusza

Enslow Publishers, Inc.

40 Industrial Road   PO Box 38
Box 398   Aldershot
Berkeley Heights, NJ 07922   Hants GU12 6BP
USA   UK

http://www.enslow.com

Library of Congress Cataloging-in-Publication Data

Pietrusza, David.
    The Cleveland Indians baseball team / David Pietrusza.
       p. cm. — (Great sports teams)
    Includes bibliographical references and index.
    Summary: Surveys the history of the Cleveland Indians, covering some of
the key players and coaches and some of the best games the team has played.
    ISBN 0-7660-1491-6
    1. Cleveland Indians (Baseball team)—History—Juvenile literature.
    [1. Cleveland Indians (Baseball team)—History. 2. Baseball—History.]
    I. Title. II. Series.
GV875.C7 P564   2001
796.357'64'0977132—dc21

                                      00-009115

Printed in the United States of America

10 9 8 7 6 5 4 3 2 1

To Our Readers: All Internet Addresses in this book were active and appropriate
when we went to press. Any comments or suggestions can be sent by e-mail to
Comments@enslow.com or to the address on the back cover.

Illustration Credits: AP / Wide World Photos.

Cover Illustration: AP / Wide World Photos.

Cover Description: Indians celebrate 1995 AL Pennant.

CONTENTS

Pitcher Bob Feller was a seventeen-year-old high school student when he made his first major-league start for the Cleveland Indians on August 25, 1936.

RAPID ROBERT

Bob Feller was a special kind of rookie. In 1936, Feller, a seventeen-year-old Iowa farm boy, was the talk of baseball. There had been other great prospects before, but Feller was at another level. He was still only in high school, but here he was about to appear in the major leagues—not just with a chance to stay on the big club's roster. Some thought he had a chance to be one of the best ever.

Major-League News

In July of that year, he had made his debut for the American League (AL)'s Cleveland Indians in an exhibition game against the National League (NL)'s St. Louis Cardinals. In three innings of relief work, he struck out 8 Cardinals. From that moment on, Feller was major-league news. He made a few more relief outings. Then in mid-August, Indians manager Steve O'Neill gave Feller his first big-league start.

What a start it was. The seventeen-year-old struck out 15 St. Louis Browns in a 4–1 victory. Feller was the first American League pitcher to strike out 15 in a game, since Yankees right-hander Bob Shawkey had done this in 1919. Feller had missed the AL strikeout record by just a single whiff.

Pitcher's Duel

Steve O'Neill continued to start the young right-hander. On Sunday, September 13, 1936, the Indians were scheduled to play a doubleheader. Cleveland's opponent was the Philadelphia Athletics led by legendary manager Connie Mack. The game was at Cleveland's old stadium, League Park. Feller would be starting the first game on that overcast afternoon. About six thousand fans paid their way in to see a duel between Feller and the A's eighteen-year-old right-hander, Randy Gumbert. Feller's fastball was taking off on virtually every pitch, moving up and down, out or in. Against a lineup like the free-swinging A's, he should have been particularly effective.

He was. "You've got it today!" shouted Cleveland catcher "Greek" George.[1] Yes, he had it—surrendering just two hits to the A's—but he had too much of it. Philadelphia batters were striking out in droves, but Feller was as wild as a pitcher could be. He walked 9 batters. He threw a wild pitch and hit A's right fielder Wally Moses. Philadelphia ran wild on the basepaths,

*I*ndians manager Steve O'Neill (left) gave Feller (right) the ball for his first starting assignment.

taking advantage of the young Feller's high kick, stealing 9 bases.

Going into the ninth inning, "the Tribe," as the Indians are commonly known, led, 5–2. Feller struck out at least one Athletic in every inning except for the fourth. Twice he had struck out the side. By the end of the sixth he had 12 strikeouts. He fanned two more in both the seventh and eighth innings. That added up to 16 strikeouts, tying Rube Waddell's twenty-eight-year-old AL record, and leaving him one shy of the major-league record set a few years earlier by Dizzy Dean of the St. Louis Cardinals.

Will the Record Be Broken

Feller was tiring. After all, he had thrown a lot of pitches. He retired Philadelphia catcher Frankie Hayes on a pop fly. Then Charlie Moss pinch hit for Randy Gumbert and walked. He then swiped the ninth base off Feller and catcher "Greek" George. Left fielder George Puccinelli was up next. He had struck out twice already. This time he worked the count full, to three balls and two strikes.

Bob Feller towels off in the dressing room after setting a new strikeout record against the Philadelphia Athletics on September 13, 1936. Feller struck out 17 in the game.

"Greek" George walked to the mound. He wanted to calm Feller down. "What do you think on this one?" asked George.

"He will be looking for the fast ball," said Feller, "Let's make it a curve."[2]

Feller wound up. "I cut loose with everything I had and Puccinelli took it. Strike three—called."[3]

"You're out [of] there," yelled plate umpire Lou Kolls.[4] Seventeen-year-old Robert William Andrew Feller was in the record books. More than that, he was on the road to being perhaps Cleveland's greatest player ever.

Pitcher Satchel Paige, one of the greatest players in the Negro Leagues, joined the Cleveland Indians in 1948.

A PROUD TRADITION

Major-league baseball in Cleveland dates back to May 4, 1871, when the Forest City Club of Cleveland played in the very first game of the National Association, the very first major league.

Early Cleveland Clubs

The city later boasted teams in the early National League, in the major-league American Association, and in the Players League. In the 1890s, the Cleveland Spiders were among the National League's best teams. Owner Frank DeHaas Robison moved the team's best talent to the St. Louis Cardinals (which he also owned), and his Cleveland club fell apart, losing 134 games in 1898. The Spiders went out of business at season's end.

The major leagues returned to Cleveland when Ban Johnson formed the American League in 1901.

The new team was called the Blues, and later the Bronchos, the Naps (after star player Napoleon "Larry" Lajoie), and finally the Indians. This time the team was named for former Cleveland outfielder Louis Sockalexis, a Penobscot Indian from Maine.

A Sad Day

The Indians started to jell only after acquiring center fielder Tris Speaker from the Boston Red Sox in 1916. In 1920, three star right-handed pitchers—Jim Bagby (who won a team-record 31 games), Hall of Famer Stanley Covaleski, and Ray Caldwell—starred for the team. Cleveland won the AL pennant in a close battle with the White Sox and Yankees. It was, nonetheless, a very difficult year for the club. Late in the season, popular Indians shortstop Ray Chapman was hit in the head by a pitch from Yankees pitcher Carl Mays. Chapman became the only major-leaguer ever to die from an on-field injury. The Indians replaced Chapman with future Hall of Famer Joe Sewell.

The Indians faced the Brooklyn Robins in the 1920 Fall Classic, one of the most historic of all World Series. In Game 5, Indians outfielder Elmer Smith became the first player to hit a World Series grand slam. In that same game, Cleveland second baseman Bill Wambsganss became the first—and to this date, only—player to turn an unassisted triple play in World Series competition.

In the next two decades, the Indians featured many fine players. Pitchers Mel Harder, Wes Ferrell, and Bob Feller, slugging first baseman Hal Trosky, and Hall of

Fame outfielder Earl Averill spurred the team. Still, the Indians did not win any pennants.

Winning Ways

Not until flamboyant Bill Veeck, Jr., took over the club in the mid-1940s would the Indians return to glory. Veeck knew how to promote. He also knew how to build a good team. He signed two great Negro Leaguers—pitcher Satchel Paige and slugger Larry Doby. Despite some initial doubts, he kept the player-manager, shortstop Lou Boudreau, on the job. Hitters

Larry Doby batted .318 in the 1948 World Series as the Indians defeated the Boston Braves, four games to two. Doby was the first African-American player in the AL.

such as second baseman Bobby Avila and third baseman Al Rosen anchored the offense.

The Indians defeated the Red Sox in a one-game playoff to win the 1948 AL pennant. In the World Series that fall, the Tribe defeated the Boston Braves in six games, as right-hander Bob Lemon won two games and Doby batted .318.

Third baseman Al Rosen's 32 home runs and 126 RBI helped the Indians win 111 games during the 1954 season.

The Cleveland Indians Baseball Team

Record Setting Year

Veeck and Boudreau moved on, but the Indians had another pennant left in them. Al Lopez took over as manager and delivered a pennant in 1954 as the team compiled a then-league-record 111 games. Avila led the league with a .341 average. Rosen led the league with 32 homers and 126 RBIs. Hall of Fame right-hander Early Wynn won 23 games.

In the World Series, the Indians lost their magic touch. Willie Mays and the New York Giants swept them in four games. The team continued to contend in the 1950s—but trouble was brewing. A young, hard-throwing pitcher named Herb Score seemed like the next Bob Feller. Then, on May 7, 1957, Yankees infielder Gil McDougald lined a pitch straight at Score's head. Score was never the same. The Indians also had two fine young hard-hitting outfielders—Roger Maris and Rocky Colavito. Cleveland fans really loved Colavito. The team traded Maris to the Kansas City Athletics and Colavito to the Detroit Tigers.

For decades, the Indians would post losing records. Some said it was the "Curse of Rocky Colavito." It would take a long time to undo that curse.

*B**ob Feller retired as the Cleveland Indians all-time leader in wins, shutouts, innings pitched, and strikeouts.*

INDIANS IMMORTALS

The Indians have boasted many fine players in their long history. Many are in the National Baseball Hall of Fame in Cooperstown, New York. Others, such as outfielder Rocky Colavito and first baseman Jim Thome, rank among the most feared sluggers of their time.

Napoleon "Larry" Lajoie

Second baseman Larry Lajoie was not only the Indians' first great star—he was also the first great star of the new American League. His .426 average in 1901 remains the American League record. For a while, the Indians were even called the Naps in his honor. *Total Baseball: The Official Encyclopedia of Major League Baseball* ranks him second in Total Player Ranking—behind only Babe Ruth. Lajoie was named to the Hall of Fame in 1937.

Addie Joss

Most fans today do not recognize the name Addie Joss, but he may have been the greatest Indians pitcher of them all. His lifetime ERA of 1.88 is the second best in baseball history. He pitched 45 shutouts and completed 90 percent of his starts. His career record was 160–97. "Addie can put a curveball exactly where a batter can't hit it nines times out of ten," said Tigers immortal Ty Cobb.[1] Cobb meant what he said—he batted just .071 against Joss. Tragically, the pitcher died of tubercular meningitis in 1910, at the age of thirty-one. He was elected to the Hall of Fame in 1978.

Tris Speaker

Tris Speaker is fifth all-time, with a .345 lifetime batting average. He may have been best known, however, for his great play in the outfield. "You can talk about Willie Mays and Joe DiMaggio and all the other great center fielders you want," contended teammate Joe Sewell, "but none of them, and I mean none of them, could carry Tris Speaker's glove."[2] He was named to the Hall of Fame in 1937.

Bob Feller

"I was a bonus baby," Feller once noted. "I got two autographed baseballs and a scorecard from the 1935 All-Star Game."[3] "Rapid Robert" is still the Indians' all-time leader in wins (266), shutouts (46), innings pitched (3,827), and strikeouts (2,581). Partly to honor his World War II service, in 1997 the Society for American Baseball Research bestowed on him its first

Hero of Baseball Award. The team retired his uniform number nineteen, the first number retired by the club, in 1957. He was named to the Hall of Fame in 1962.

Early Wynn

Pitcher Early "Gus" Wynn was tough—a fierce competitor. Once Wynn invited the great Ted Williams to go fishing with him in the Everglades. "Admit it," said Wynn. "You're afraid to go into the Everglades with me."

Pitcher Early Wynn won 300 games in his career and won twenty games or more five different seasons.

"No hitter ever would go into the Everglades with a pitcher like you," Williams responded. "His body might never be found."[4]

Wynn was not only tough—he was very good. He won 300 games in his career and had five twenty-win seasons. Four of those seasons were with the Indians. In 1954, he led the American League with 23 wins. In 1950, he led the AL with a 3.20 ERA, and in 1957, he led the circuit with 184 strikeouts. Wynn won election to the Hall of Fame in 1972.

Rocky Colavito

Rocky Colavito was the power hitter Indians fans had always dreamed of. In 1958, he batted .303 with 41 homers and 113 RBIs. In 1959, he slammed 42 homers, to tie for the AL lead in that category. "He was young, handsome, and hit a lot of home runs," remembered one fan decades later. "They talk about being like Michael Jordan today. In Cleveland in 1959 it was 'be like Rocky.'"[5] Cleveland fans were outraged when Colavito went to the Tigers in exchange for batting champion Harvey Kuenn. The Tribe later re-acquired Colavito. In 1965, he led the AL with 93 walks and 108 RBIs for Cleveland.

Jim Thome

Infielder Jim Thome is a manager's dream. He combines great talent with a great attitude. When the team acquired slugging third baseman Matt Williams from the Giants in 1997 and moved Thome from third base to first, Thome did not complain. He just kept on

The Cleveland Indians Baseball Team

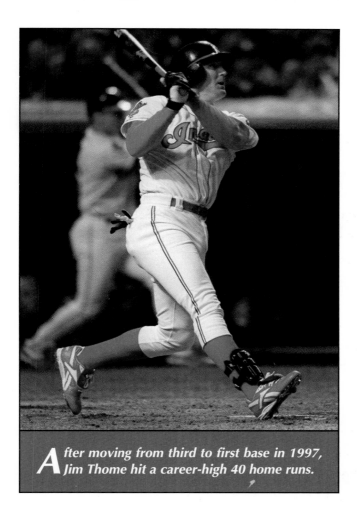

*A*fter moving from third to first base in 1997, Jim Thome hit a career-high 40 home runs.

hitting. That year he slugged a career-high 40 homers. In the 1998 postseason, he put on an impressive power display. In the Division Series, he homered twice, then added four more dingers in the ALCS. In 1999, he had another fine year, with 33 homers and 108 RBIs.

*I*ndians owner Bill Veeck ran many exciting promotions to bring fans to the ballpark. He was elected to baseball's Hall of Fame in 1991.

INDIANS MANAGEMENT

The Indians have had many outstanding managers. Some, like Tris Speaker, Lou Boudreau, and Al Lopez, have won election to Baseball's Hall of Fame. So has Indians owner Bill Veeck.

Bill Veeck

With the exception of the winning teams of the 1990s, the happiest time in Indians history was when Bill Veeck owned the team. Veeck bought the club after World War II and ran many exciting promotions to attract fans. "Back before Bill stirred up the pot," said long-time Veeck associate Rudy Schaffer, "the biggest promotion in the major leagues was to open up the gates and say we're playing at three."[1] In 1948, the team attracted 2,620,627 fans—a major-league record that lasted for over three decades. There was more to Bill Veeck than just hoopla. He was also capable of building great teams, and in 1948 he delivered Cleveland's first pennant in twenty-eight years. Veeck was elected to the Hall of Fame in 1991.

Lou Boudreau

Boudreau started with the club as a slick fielding third baseman, and then moved over to shortstop. "They say [Joe] DiMaggio was the greatest clutch hitter," Hall of Fame Yankee manager Joe McCarthy once observed. "Well, maybe Boudreau was the greatest clutch fielder."[2] In 1941, while still in his twenties, Boudreau asked to be considered for the Indians' managership. Much to his surprise, he got the job. In 1944, he led the American League in batting, with a .327 average. In 1948, he managed the team to a world championship. Boudreau, later a Cubs announcer, won election to the Hall of Fame in 1970.

Al Lopez

Lopez, a former slick-fielding catcher, replaced Boudreau in 1951. He was a great handler of pitchers and pioneered the development of the Indians bullpen with relievers Ray Narleski and Don Mossi. In 1954, Lopez led the Indians to a then-record 111 wins. He later went on to manage the White Sox to the pennant in 1959 (under Bill Veeck, who had also moved on to Chicago) and won election to the Hall of Fame in 1977.

Frank Robinson

In 1977, the Indians hired the first African-American manager in major-league history, former Reds and Orioles star Frank Robinson. Robinson was one of the

The Cleveland Indians Baseball Team

*F*rank Robinson became the first African-American manager in baseball when the Indians hired him in 1977.

game's greatest hitters—and one of its fiercest competitors. "The thing about Frank is that he hates to lose," said second baseman Joe Morgan. "And Frank makes it very uncomfortable to be around if you do lose. A lot of people say they hate to lose, but they don't really mean it. Frank does."[3]

*M*ike Hargrove argues a call with umpire Joe Brinkman during the 1998 Division Series. Hargrove led the Indians to five consecutive division titles.

Mike Hargrove

As a player, first baseman Mike Hargrove was known as "the Human Rain Delay" because of way he prolonged each at-bat.[4] It drove fans crazy, but whatever he was doing must have worked, because he hit .290 over the course of his major-league career. Whatever he did as Indians manager must also have worked. In 1995, he led the team to a 100–44 record and the Tribe's first World Series appearance since 1954. Under Hargrove, the team captured division

The Cleveland Indians Baseball Team

titles each year from 1995 through 1999 and won AL pennants in 1995 and 1997. Despite his success, Hargrove was fired by General Manager Jim Hart after losing the 1999 ALCS to Boston. Hart was displeased by Hargrove's failure to raise the team to the "next level."[5] Hargrove was quickly hired by the Baltimore Orioles as their manager.

*M*any Indians fans believe the team was "cursed" after they traded Rocky Colavito to the Tigers in 1960. Colavito had been extremely popular with the Cleveland faithful.

THE CURSE OF ROCKY COLAVITO

For most of their history, the Cleveland Indians had been one of baseball's more competitive and likable teams. True, they had won only three pennants—but when you are in the same league as the New York Yankees, three pennants is a respectable total. Also, the team had usually finished in the American League's first division. They had finished last only in 1914.

Rock Bottom

All that seemed to change with the trade of Rocky Colavito to the Tigers in 1960. It was probably just a coincidence, but in 1960 the Indians went into a long period of decline, becoming one of the worst teams in the league.

In 1960, the team sank from second to fourth, posting its first losing record since 1946. The Tribe recorded a third-place finish (86–75) in 1968 under

Hall of Fame pitcher Gaylord Perry was one of the few bright spots for the Indians during the 1970s.

manager Alvin Dark. In 1976, the Indians finished fourth, 81–78, under Frank Robinson. A sixth-place finish (81–80) in 1979 under Jeff Torborg and Dave Garcia, and a fifth-place finish (84–78) in 1984 under manager Pat Corrales, were respectable. But in every other season from 1960 through 1993, Cleveland recorded a losing mark.

In all those years, the club never finished closer than 11 games back. In 1969, the Indians finished a whopping 49½ games back.

It was an ugly period in Cleveland baseball history. Unknowns like first baseman Bob Chance (.279 in 1964) or outfielder Ted Uhlaender (.288 in 1972) might lead the team in batting, or outfielder Max Alvis might pace it with just 67 RBIs in 1963.

Chief Indians

Yet the team also had its share of good players. Occasionally the team might boast an outstanding pitcher. These include "Sudden Sam" McDowell, Hall of Famer Gaylord Perry, Luis Tiant, Dennis Eckersley, or Bert Blyleven. The hard-throwing McDowell might have turned out to be the best of the bunch, and one of the greatest pitchers ever. But he squandered his opportunity by drinking heavily. "As it turned out my talent was a curse," he later said. "The curse was the way I handled it and didn't handle it."[1]

There were some good hitters as well. Slick-fielding third baseman Graig Nettles patrolled the Cleveland hot corner before moving on to the Yankees. Second baseman Julio Franco provided quality work for the Tribe in the 1980s. First baseman Andre Thornton led the team in homers each year from 1977 through 1979.

And then there was Joe Charboneau, known as "Super Joe." If anyone personified the frustration of Indians baseball back then, it was this colorful 1980 AL Rookie of the Year. On Opening Day at Cleveland's Municipal Stadium, Charboneau singled, doubled, and homered. He batted .289 for the year, with 23 homers and 87 RBIs. Super Joe looked like he might lead Cleveland out of the second-division wilderness.

Instead, by the middle of the next season he was back in the minors. Two back operations later, he was out of baseball completely.

Bad Luck

All sorts of problems seemed to strike the Indians. Max Alvis came down with spinal meningitis. "I played, but I wasn't the same player," said Alvis. "I just wasn't as strong physically. It had been a real shock to my system."[2] Outfielder Walt Bond, who many thought would be the next Colavito, died of

Sandy Alomar was one of the main reasons for the Indians rise to the top of the standings in the 1990s. Alomar was Most Valuable Player of the 1997 All-Star Game.

leukemia in 1967. First baseman Tony Horton drove in 93 runs in his rookie season in 1969, but in the following year the pressure got to him. He suffered a nervous breakdown and was soon out of the game. Catcher Ray Fosse was bowled over by Pete Rose at the 1970 All-Star game, hurt his shoulder, and was never the same.

Terrible Accidents

Then, in spring training of 1993, just as it appeared that the Tribe's luck was finally about to turn, pitchers Tim Crews and Steve Olin died in a tragic boating accident. Fellow hurler Bobby Ojeda was severely injured. That November another Indians pitcher, Cliff Young, perished in an auto accident.

It was the darkness before the dawn. The greatest Cleveland era was about to begin.

*O*utfielder Kenny Lofton's speed on the base paths helped lead the Indians to a 100-win season in 1995.

HOME-FIELD ADVANTAGE

In the second half of the 1992 season, the Cleveland Indians had played terrific ball. Sadly, the death of pitchers Tim Crews and Steve Olin, and the injury to Bob Ojeda, cast a pall on their 1993 season. It would be their last in cavernous old Municipal Stadium.

Home Sweet Home

In 1994, the Tribe would unveil beautiful new Jacobs Field, named after owner Richard Jacobs. The new stadium gave the city of Cleveland a new sense of civic pride—and the way the Indians were playing in their new home was not hurting either.

Led by outfielders Albert Belle (36 home runs, 101 RBIs, .357) and Kenny Lofton (.349 and a league-leading 60 stolen bases), the 1994 Indians missed winning the AL's new Central Division by just a single game. When the 1995 season opened, the club came roaring out of the gate and never looked back. The tribe posted a 100–44 record, winning the division by a full thirty games. Albert Belle dominated the league, leading its batters with 50 homers, 52 doubles, 121 runs scored, and a .690 slugging average. Belle became the first player ever to have 50 doubles and 50 homers in the same season. Kenny Lofton led the AL with 13 triples and 54 stolen bases. Jose Mesa paced the circuit with 46 saves.

Into the Series

The Indians swept Boston in the first round of the playoffs, then squeaked by the Mariners in an exciting ALCS. Cleveland pitcher Orel Hershiser won both of his starts, posted a gleaming 1.29 ERA in the ALCS and captured ALCS MVP honors. In the World Series, however, manager Mike Hargrove's team lost to Atlanta in six contests.

Cleveland fans, who had not seen a World Series since 1954, appreciated the club's efforts. Before the 1996 season began, the club sold out every seat in Jacobs Field—the first time in baseball history that this had happened anywhere. The Indians captured the AL Central Division once again in 1996 (as Lofton once again led the AL in stolen bases), but fell to the wildcard Baltimore Orioles, three games to one, in the division series.

In 1997, Cleveland took the AL Central for the third straight time. The Tribe edged the Yankees, 3–2, in the division series and beat Baltimore, 4–2, in the ALCS, despite hitting only .193 as a team.

The Cleveland Indians Baseball Team

In that year's World Series, they faced the upstart Florida Marlins. The Tribe came within two outs of nailing down the Fall Classic but lost to Florida, 3–2, in eleven innings on a bases-loaded single by shortstop Edgar Renteria off Cleveland's Charles Nagy.

String of Success

By now, winning their division was old hat for Cleveland. They won again in 1998 behind Manny

In 1995, Manny Ramirez emerged as one of the top hitters in baseball. He combined for a spectacular total of 310 RBIs in 1998 and 1999.

Ramirez (45 home runs, 145 RBIs) and Gold Glove shortstop Omar Vizquel. The Indians demolished Boston, 3–1, in the division series, but lost the ALCS to Joe Torre's powerful (114–48) Yankees.

It was more of the same in 1999 as the Indians (97–65) captured their division by 21½ games. Team leaders included Manny Ramirez (44 home runs, 165 RBIs, .333), Roberto Alomar (24 home runs, 120 RBIs,

Bartolo Colon's 18 victories helped lead the Indians to the 1999 Central Division crown.

The Cleveland Indians Baseball Team

.323), Jim Thome (33 home runs, 108 RBIs) and Bartolo Colon (18–5, 3.95 ERA). Ramirez's RBI total was the highest in the majors since 1938. The team jumped off to quick two-games-to-none lead in the division series against Boston, but were stunned when the Red Sox came back to win in five games. Included was a shocking 23–7 rout in Game 4.

A New Direction

The off-season saw some changes for the franchise. Popular Indians batting coach Charlie Manuel replaced Mike Hargrove as manager, and local cable-television magnate Larry Dolan purchased the team for $320 million from Richard Jacobs—reportedly the highest price ever paid for a baseball team.

That translates into a big change at the top, but with sound management and solid fan support, the Indians should continue their winning ways.

STATISTICS

The Indians History

YEARS	W	L	PCT.	PENNANTS	WORLD SERIES
1901–09	697	632	.524	None	None
1910–19	742	747	.498	None	None
1920–29	786	749	.512	1920	1920
1930–39	824	708	.538	None	None
1940–49	800	731	.523	1948	1948
1950–59	904	634	.588	1954	None
1960–69	783	826	.487	None	None
1970–79	737	866	.460	None	None
1980–89	710	849	.455	None	None
1990–99	823	728	.531	1995, 1997	None
2000–	90	72	.556	None	None

The Indians Today

YEAR	W	L	PCT.	MANAGER	DIVISION FINISH
1991	57	105	.352	John McNamara, Mike Hargrove	7
1992	76	86	.469	Mike Hargrove	4 (tie)
1993	76	86	.469	Mike Hargrove	6
1994	66	47	.584	Mike Hargrove	2
1995	100	44	.694	Mike Hargrove	1
1996	99	62	.615	Mike Hargrove	1
1997	86	75	.534	Mike Hargrove	1
1998	89	73	.549	Mike Hargrove	1
1999	97	65	.599	Mike Hargrove	1
2000	90	72	.556	Charlie Manuel	2

Total History

W	L	PCT.	PENNANTS	WORLD SERIES
7,896	7,542	.511	5	2

W=Wins   L=Losses   PCT.=Winning Percentage   PENNANTS=Won league title
WORLD SERIES=Won World Series

Championship Managers

MANAGER	YEARS MANAGED	RECORD	CHAMPIONSHIPS
Tris Speaker	1919–26	616–520	World Series, 1920
Lou Boudreau	1942–50	728–649	World Series, 1948
Al Lopez	1951–56	570–354	AL Pennant, 1954
Mike Hargrove	1991–99	721–591	AL Pennant, 1995, 1997

Great Hitters

PLAYER	SEA	CAREER STATISTICS								
		YRS	G	AB	R	H	HR	RBI	SB	AVG
Albert Belle	1989–96	12	1,539	5,853	974	1,726	381	1,239	88	.295
Lou Boudreau*	1938–50	15	1,646	6,029	861	1,779	68	789	51	.295
Rocky Colavito	1955–59 1965–67	14	1,841	6,503	971	1,730	374	1,159	19	.266
Larry Doby*	1947–55 1958	13	1,533	5,348	960	1,515	253	970	47	.283
Joe Jackson	1910–15	13	1,332	4,981	873	1,772	54	785	202	.356
Nap Lajoie*	1902–14	21	2,480	9,589	1,504	3,242	82	1,599	380	.338
Manny Ramirez	1993–00	8	967	3,470	665	1,086	236	804	28	.313
Joe Sewell*	1920–30	14	1,903	7,132	1,141	2,226	49	1,055	74	.312
Tris Speaker*	1916–26	22	2,789	10,195	1,882	3,514	117	1,529	432	.345
Jim Thome	1991–	10	1,074	3,634	715	1,033	233	685	17	.284

SEA=Seasons with Indians
YRS=Years in the Majors
G=Games
AB=At-Bats
R=Runs Scored
H=Hits
HR=Home Runs
RBI=Runs Batted In
SB=Stolen Bases
AVG=Batting Average
*Member of National Baseball Hall of Fame

Career Statistics

Great Pitchers

PLAYER	SEA	CAREER STATISTICS									
		YRS	W	L	PCT	ERA	G	SV	IP	K	SH
Stanley Covaleski*	1916–24	14	215	142	.602	2.89	450	21	3,082	981	3:
Bob Feller*	1936–41 1945–56	18	266	162	.621	3.25	570	21	3,827	2,581	4:
Addie Joss*	1902–10	9	160	97	.623	1.89	286	5	2,327	920	4!
Bob Lemon*	1946–58	13	207	128	.618	3.23	460	22	2,850	1,277	3:
Early Wynn*	1949–57 1963	23	300	244	.551	3.54	691	15	4,564	2,334	4!

SEA=Seasons with Indians
YRS=Years in the Majors
W=Wins
L=Losses

PCT=Winning Percentage
ERA=Earned Run Average
G=Games
SV=Saves

IP=Innings Pitched
K=Strikeouts
SH=Shutouts

*Member of National Baseball Hall of Fame

The Cleveland Indians Baseball Team

CHAPTER NOTES

Chapter 1. Rapid Robert

1. Bob Feller, *Strikeout Story* (New York: A. S. Barnes & Co., 1947), p. 56.
2. Ibid., p. 57.
3. Bob Feller with Bill Gilbert, *Now Pitching: Bob Feller* (New York: Birch Lane Press, 1990), p. 30.
4. Feller, *Strikeout Story*, p. 57.

Chapter 3. Indians Immortals

1. Scott Longert, *Addie Joss: King of the Pitchers* (Cleveland: Society for American Baseball Research, 1998), p. 107.
2. Nathan Salant, *Superstars, Stars, and Just Plain Heroes* (New York: Stein & Day, 1982), p. 47.
3. Bob Chiger, ed., *Voices of Baseball: Quotations on the Summer Game* (New York: Signet, 1983), p. 128.
4. John Thorn et al., eds., *Total Indians* (New York: Penguin Books, 1996), p. 77.
5. Terry Pluto, *The Curse of Rocky Colavito: A Loving Look at a Thirty-Year Slump* (New York: Fireside, 1995), p. 40.

Chapter 4. Indians Management

1. John Thorn et al., eds., *Total Indians* (New York: Penguin Books, 1996), p. 75.
2. Donald Honig, *The Greatest Shortstops of All Time* (Dubuque, Iowa: Elysian Fields Press, 1992), p. 50.
3. Frank Robinson and Berry Stainback, *Extra Innings* (New York: McGraw Hill, 1988), p. 174.
4. John Thorn et al., eds., *Total Baseball*, 6th edition (New York: Total Sports, 1999), p. 157.
5. Associated Press, "Hargrove Takes Fall for Tribe Failure," *New York Post*, October 16, 1999, p. 44.

Chapter 5. The Curse of Rocky Colavito

1. Paul Dickson, *Baseball's Greatest Quotations* (New York: HarperCollins, 1991), p. 283.
2. Terry Pluto, *The Curse of Rocky Colavito: A Loving Look at a Thirty-Year Slump* (New York: Fireside, 1995), p. 117.

GLOSSARY

American Association—A defunct major league that operated from 1882 through 1891. Not to be confused with a later minor league by the same name.

American League—One of the two current major leagues of baseball, founded in 1901 by Ban Johnson. The other major league is the National League. The primary difference between the two leagues is that since 1973 the American League (AL) has used the designated hitter rule.

batting average—At-bats divided by hits.

bonus baby—A player that receives additional money or perks, simply for signing a contract.

Cooperstown—The town in upstate New York that is the home of Baseball's Hall of Fame. At one time it was believed that baseball was invented in Cooperstown.

Cy Young Award—Award given each year to the best pitcher in each major league.

designated hitter—A player who bats, but who does not take the field during the game. In the major leagues, the designated hitter (DH) is used only in American League ballparks.

division series—The first round of the postseason.

ERA (Earned Run Average)—The number of earned runs divided by the number of innings pitched times nine; the ERA is perhaps the best measure of pitching effectiveness.

first division—Being in the first half of club's in the league or division according to won-lost percentage; usually but not always that translates into having a winning record.

free agent—A major-leaguer whose contractual obligations to his old team have expired and who is free to sign with any major-league team.

general manager—The official in charge of a ball club's business and personnel matters.

Gold Glove Award—Award given annually to the best fielder at each position in both the National and American leagues.

Hall of Fame—Located in Cooperstown, New York. Membership in the National Baseball Hall of Fame is the highest honor that can be awarded to a professional player.

homer—Home run.

infielder—One who plays an infield position (first, second, or third base or shortstop).

League Championship Series—The best-of-seven series that determines the American and National League champions.

MVP Award (Most Valuable Player award)—voted on by members of the Baseball Writers Association of America (BBWAA).

National Association—The first major league. It operated from 1871 through 1875.

National League—The oldest surviving major league, founded in 1876 by William Hulbert. Sometimes called the senior circuit.

pennant—A league championship, alternately called the flag.

RBI—Run batted in.

rookie—A first-year player.

Players League—A rival major league. It operated in only one year, 1890.

Rookie of the Year Award—Award given each year to an outstanding rookie in each major league. It was first awarded in 1947, to the Dodgers' Jackie Robinson.

second division—Being in the second half of club's in the league or division according to won-lost percentage; usually, but not always, that translates into having a losing record.

stolen base—A play in which the base runner advances to another base while the pitcher takes his motion.

wildcard—The nondivision winning club with the best won-lost percentage in regular-season play; the wildcard team in each league earns a berth in postseason play.

World Series—The end-of-season best-of-seven series that pits the champions of the National and American Leagues against each other.

FURTHER READING

Boudreau, Lou, with Russell Schneider, *Lou Boudreau: Covering All the Bases*. Champaigne, Ill.: Sagamore, 1993.

Eckhouse, Morris, *Bob Feller*. New York: Chelsea House, 1990.

Feller, Bob, with Bill Gilbert, *Now Pitching: Bob Feller*. New York: Birch Lane Press, 1990.

Manoloff, Dennis, *Omar Vizquel: The Man With the Golden Glove*. Champaigne Ill.: Sports Publishing, Inc., 1999.

Paige, Satchel, as told to Hal Lebovitz, *Pitchin' Man: Satchel Paige's Own Story*. Westport, Conn.: Meckler, 1992.

Pluto, Terry, *The Curse of Rocky Colavito: A Loving Look at a Thirty-Year Slump*. New York: Fireside, 1995.

Robinson, Frank, and Berry Stainback, *Extra Innings*. New York: McGraw Hill, 1988.

Schneider, Russell, *The Cleveland Indians Encyclopedia*. Philadelphia: Temple University Press, 1996.

Singletary, Wes, *Al Lopez: The Life of Baseball's El Senor*. Jefferson, N.C.: McFarland & Co., 1999.

Stewart, Mark, *Kenny Lofton: Man of Steal*. Chicago: Children's Press, 1998.

Thorn, John, et al., eds. *Total Baseball*. Sixth edition. New York: Total Sports, 1999.

——————, et al., eds. *Total Indians*. New York: Penguin, 1996.

Torry, Jack, *Endless Summers: The Fall and Rise of the Cleveland Indians*. South Bend, Ind.: Diamond Communications, 1996.

Tuttle, Dennis R., *Albert Belle*. Broomall, Pa.: Chelsea House, 1997.

INDEX

WHERE TO WRITE AND INTERNET SITES

Official Page of the Cleveland Indians
http://www.indians.com

Cleveland Indians at CBS Sportsline
http://cbs.sportsline.com/u/
baseball/mlb/teams/CLE/
index.html

Bob Feller's Hall of Fame Bio
http://baseballhalloffame.org/
hofers_and_honorees/hofer_bios/feller_bob.htm

Cleveland Indians
Jacobs Field
2401 Ontario Street
Cleveland, Ohio 44115

The Cleveland Indians Baseball Team